Hu-Ubuntu
I Am Because We Are

by Patrick Makokoro

Illustrated by Danika Runyan

tellwell

Tellwell Talent
www.tellwell.ca

To my parents, for values.

Pana is excited to fly on an airplane from his warm home in Zimbabwe, Africa all the way to Canada, to join his dad.

Pana looks forward to seeing snow for the first time, making a snowman, snow angels and having snowball fights with his family.

He arrives in cold Victoria, British Columbia right in the middle of winter. His momma made sure he had warm gloves, a heavy jacket and a woolen toque.

Pana is excited to go to school and make new friends.

He wonders how his class will look and how many friends he might make. What is playtime like in Canada?

In school, Pana notices that not everyone likes to play with him. They ask in mean voices, "What are you doing here? Why are you eating our food? Why don't you go back to Africa?"

Pana stays quiet. He thinks that if he tells a grown up, he might never make any friends.

A boy called Peter hits Pana and says even meaner things to him.

Every day Pana feels so alone and hurt until the day Jay comes to school.

Jay is very friendly; he doesn't care what other kids say about Pana. In fact, he plays with Pana and becomes his buddy.

Pana and Jay soon become best friends.

Even though they are different, they share laughter, dreams, and adventures.

As they grow, their friendship deepens, and other kids learn to be more loving and accepting because of them.

As their friendship grows, many children see: true friendship can happen no matter the shade of our skin.

So many kids want to be a part of their
happy group that welcomes everyone.

Because of this, other kids get the chance to share their stories of where they came from.

Their laughter and acceptance fills the school with joy and understanding.

These friends know that love and being
included are powerful feelings that bring
people together.

20

No matter how different
we are, love and respect
weave us together.

We can learn to rise above
our differences.

Pana shares with Jay about Hu-Ubuntu: I am because we are.

Pana imagines a beautiful world filled
with love and understanding.

As the children play together, they learn new traditions and their friendships become stronger.

All races and cultures can live peacefully as one family, loving our differences, and sharing our beautiful cultures.

I am because we are!

A Note from the Author

This book tells a story of the importance of kindness, compassion, and interconnectedness reign supreme. This book is an invitation to explore the beautiful concept of Hu-Ubuntu, a philosophy rooted in the belief that "I am because we are." Derived from the Shona word Hunhu in Zimbabwe and Zulu word Ubuntu in South Africa the name Hu-Ubuntu coined by the Author brings to the fore the importance of wellness and relatability.

Hu-Ubuntu teaches us that we are all connected, that our individual well-being is intertwined with the well-being of our community. It reminds us that our actions have a ripple effect, impacting not only ourselves but also those around us.

Through the stories and illustrations in this Hu-Ubuntu Children's book series, we will embark on a journey to discover the essence of Hu-Ubuntu. We will meet characters who embody this philosophy, demonstrating acts of generosity, empathy, and collaboration. We will learn how small gestures of kindness can create a ripple of positivity, transforming individuals and communities alike.

Hu-Ubuntu is not just a word; it's a way of life. It's about recognizing our shared humanity, celebrating our differences, and working together to create a more just and harmonious world. As you turn the pages of this book reading it, I hope you will be inspired to work with your young learners, your children, your grandchildren and those young ones in your life to embrace the spirit of Hu-Ubuntu in their own lives.

Let us teach our children to share a smile with their classmates, offer a helping hand, and remember that their actions, however small, have the power to make a difference. Together, let us build a world where Hu-Ubuntu is not just a concept but a lived reality, where we all thrive because we are connected, and our destinies are inextricably linked.

Explore further books and resources available at www.huubuntuconsulting.com.

Author Bio

Patrick Makokoro is an author and social entrepreneur. With a background as a development consultant, his interests span community development, social justice, early childhood education and child protection.

X: @PatrickMakokoro
LinkedIn: @PatrickMakokoro
Instagram: @PatrickMakokoro

www.ingramcontent.com/pod-product-compliance
Lightning Source LLC
Chambersburg PA
CBHW042157030726
47599CB00004B/770